THE IVORY

THE IVORY

PRINCE DENNY U. OMOREGIE

authorHOUSE®

AuthorHouse™
1663 Liberty Drive
Bloomington, IN 47403
www.authorhouse.com
Phone: 1-800-839-8640

Published by AuthorHouse   06/21/2012

ISBN: 978-1-4772-1399-5 (sc)
ISBN: 978-1-4772-1398-8 (hc)
ISBN: 978-1-4772-1397-1 (e)

CONTENTS

CREDITS/ACKNOWLEDGEMENT

Thanks to the Almighty God, for making it possible to complete this book. I will also like to thank the following people; my lovely wife Princess Pauline Omoregie, and beautiful children; Prince Emmanuel, Prince David and Princess Emmanuella Omoregie. Thank you Ella for keeping me on my toes to hasten the completion of this book.

I hereby acknowledge His Royal Highness Omo n'Oba n'Edo Uku Akpolokpolo Solomon Igbinoghodua Aisiokuoba Akenzua Erediauwa, My uncle Chief Nosakhare Isekhure 'The Isekhure of Benin, My father Chief Nosakhare Omoregie Egharevba 'The Uso of Benin', My mother Princess Ebun Omoregie (Nee Oshodin) my brothers and Sisters. Prince Sarkhi A. Omoregie, Prince Jude O. Omoregie, Princess Enid N. Onimowo, and Princess Tracy Oduwa Omoregie.

Credits to Louise C. Thompson who spent time editing this book to make sure it achieves its purpose. To the memories of the great Oba Ovonramwen N'ogbaisi, and to all who fought gallantly sacrificing their lives in defending the Great Benin Kingdom during the Benin Expedition in 1897.

INTRODUCTION

THE BENIN KINGDOM was an ancient African realm in the western part of Nigeria, and one that was free from British influence. Its people, the *Edo*, were fearless warriors who were rich in culture and tradition. This was a land enshrouded in mystery and legend, as all of its men and women possessed mysterious powers that had been passed unto them from their ancestors. Even the children would manifest abilities that defied science and which the human mind would struggle to comprehend. People would flock from neighbouring towns and villages just to witness the magical and spiritual might of the Edo people, who every year would host a festival known as *Isie o kuo*, meaning 'battlefront', during which they would re-enact battle scenes using real weapons. They would strike each other with machetes, shoot each other with arrows and spears, and fight with knives and swords—yet none of them were ever injured due to the magical charms they used for protection. This was just a tiny example of some of the great things the Edo were capable of doing. Their added bravery and ruthlessness in battle made them almost invincible, and they were greatly feared by those who knew them.

Despite their power and reputation, they remained lovely, hospitable people who worked hard together to protect and expand their territories. Their efforts paid off, as Benin soon became one of the fastest growing and self-reliant kingdoms in West Africa. The Edo engaged in trade by bartering with the neighbouring villages over food and cash crops. Their land was rich with cocoa, rubber, ivory, and other valuable produce such as precious corals, which were not only outstandingly beautiful but were also believed to hold divine powers of protection. As they were gotten from the ocean, corals were believed to be from the sea goddess of fertility, Olokun, and they were worn by children as bracelets and necklaces in order to ward off sickness and premature death. Adults also wore corals as a means of protection, and used them for various charms. Palm kernel, the fruit of the palm tree, was another important produce in Benin. This tree was particularly useful; every part of it, including the roots, stems, branches, leaves, nuts, and even the maggots gotten from dead and rotting branches were of value. Its reddish nuts were used to produce cooking oil, soaps, pomade creams, and many other goods, all of which contributed to the great wealth now possessed by the kingdom. It was this wealth that had recently sparked an interest from the British.

CHAPTER 1

The Gathering

ONE MID-DECEMBER EVENING, the king of Benin, known as the *Oba*, had summoned all of the villagers to come together for some entertainment. It was the Harmattan season: the days were stiflingly hot, the nights were very cold, and—as was typical for this time of year—the Edo people were suffering from the effects of the northeast wind that was blowing in from the Sahara desert. Nearly everyone in the gathering crowd was coughing; their throats were dry from inhaling the dusty air, and each person bore the bleeding, chapped lips and chaffed heels that were customary during these blustery months. Yet despite the wind, an air of fervour was bubbling amongst the people, gathering in a cloud above their heads, refusing to be blown away. Suddenly, a hush fell upon the crowd, and even the palm trees stood still. The king appeared, adorned from head to toe in royal regalia fashioned entirely from red coral, and now every pair of excited eyes was fixed on this vision of splendour. The corals had been sewn together to form a magnificent garment that hung from the neck to the ankles. Its heavy padding and imposing design added a further five inches to the king's six foot frame, and accentuated his massive physique. His head was swathed by a crown crafted entirely from coral beads and cowries in a variety of shapes, building to a tall, coral finial at the centre, from which several branches protruded. Several layers of beaded necklace were coiled from chin to chest, concealing his neck, and elaborate ropes ran in a helter-skelter right down to the bottom of the garment. Red coral bracelets dangled from the king's wrists and ankles and his shoes were encrusted with red coral beads. Finally, the skin of a leopard hung submissively from his left shoulder to remind onlookers of the power and authority in their wake. People were left in no doubt as to the spiritual powers that this entire regalia bestowed upon their king, who now was seated upon a throne swaddled in leopard furs, surveying his people.

Suddenly, a shout resonated through the stillness, so loud it sent a tingle down the spine of every man standing. It was the voice of Egele, the palace court orderly—an elderly but fit man who had also served under the previous king. For four decades, his baritone call had served to gain attention and silence in preparation for the king's speech.

"Long live the King" his voice resounded, and the crowd responded with a chorus of "*Ise*", meaning 'so be it', before dropping down flat on their stomachs and shouting "*Oba gha to okpere*" (*long live the king*).

This act of prostration was regular practice, performed to show the highest respect to the *Oba*. Once the people had arisen to their feet, the king began to speak in an imperial tone. "Thank you, my people, may the gods and my ancestors give me the wisdom to be able to rule over this land just like my fore-fathers have done from time immemorial". His voice was one that commanded instant respect, and the crowd quickly responded with their chant of "*Oba gha to okpere*".

"Today I have called you out to be entertained", the king continued, "so do enjoy yourselves".

At that moment, an old man stepped out from the crowd. His muscles rippled underneath his taut, dark skin, suggesting a level of fitness that belied his age, but as he limped slowly to the front of the gathering, it became clear that his left leg was both shorter and thinner than the right, causing him to lean in a lopsided manner as he walked. It was believed that he was born with this deformity, which had led to him being called Uke the cripple. Uke was responsible for singing the praises of the king, and he did this in a manner that no one could imitate. He had inherited the role from his forefathers, who had performed the same duty over years gone by, and now the mantle had been passed on to him by his father before he died.

"Long may you live, god amongst men, the one who gives his people life", Uke chanted in his melodic tones. "He who has never lost in a battle, and therefore knows no defeat: the pride of the Edo! May you reign forever, and may your enemies never see another day. You, O Great King, are the joy of this land. Your forefathers did rule well, but you have exceeded them because the Edo are now well known, and even children yet unborn will hear about your rule. We are feared and respected all over. We are self-sufficient and have more wealth than is necessary. This is all credited to you, my Great King. Your feet have never touched the ground; you are the greatest and most handsome being ever to be created by the gods. May you reign forever, O King!"

At this final exclamation, a roar of "*Ise*" erupted from the crowd, and the king stood up, his deep voice booming over the masses. "As you all know, we have started the *Ugi'erh'Oba Festival*, and I have received messages from the neighbouring villages asking me to reconsider their request. My response has been that I will readdress the matter after this festival, because we do not deal with such matters during this period as it is strictly for celebrations and the usual traditional rights. It is also a time when I display my generosity by distributing chieftaincy titles". As he finished speaking, there was a brilliant flash of red accompanied by a rattling of coral as the king flung his arm in the air, raising his cup in a toast to the crowd. "Now let the entertainments begin!" he shouted joyfully, and at the responding bellow of "*Oba gha to okpere*", he held his cup to the sky once more.

CHAPTER 2
The Entertainment

IN RESPONSE TO the royal command, a number of men stepped forward and began to form a line. Each stood bare-chested, showing off ripped muscles that were accentuated by the black and white paint that adorned nearly every glistening body. Some of the men wore shorts, while others had small pieces of cloth wrapped around their groins. Colourful ropes hung from each taut figure, and white smears of paint decorated each tense yet hopeful face. For these were the faces of wrestlers, each of whom was eagerly anticipating the honour of performing in front of the king, and the paint, ropes, and material were charms that gave energy and supernatural powers.

Whilst wrestling was a traditional form of entertainment for the Edo, nothing was ever as simple as it seemed in their mysterious land.

Indeed, the objective was straight-forward enough—he who got his opponent's back to touch the ground was declared the winner. However, in this kingdom, strength and technique were not enough—the use of spiritual and supernatural powers created an even greater spectacle for the onlookers. It was usually the youths of the land, including the warriors, who took part in such matches, and on occasion even some of the chiefs would participate in order to showcase their powers.

As the last wrestler took his place, the drummers began to beat a warlike rhythm. It was believed that some of the drums were spiritual: as these instruments were beaten, the fighters would become energised. As the atmosphere electrified, the crowd began to shout out the names of their favourite competitors. The main highlight of the evening was going to be the fight between the undisputed champion, Ugowe, and anyone bold enough to accept his challenge. Ugowe was nicknamed 'The Wildcat': his back had never touched the ground; he always carried a cat with him (whom he kissed before every fight); and he fought like a wild cat indeed. A soldier in the Benin army, Ugowe had never lost in a wrestling bout to anyone. The closest he had ever come to defeat was when fighting the army's leader, General Eboigbe. This match had ended as a draw—neither man had been able to get the other's back to touch the ground as they both possessed powers and techniques to counter those of each other. Now, on this mid-December evening, Ugowe was hoping to find another opponent as tough as Eboigbe because he loved a challenging fight.

Without warning, the sky darkened: threatening, black rain-clouds drifted overhead. "This might spoil our entertainment", murmured a voice in the crowd, and a few heads turned in agreement—but others knew that the king would not allow anything to jeopardise the celebration that he had arranged for his people.

Suddenly, the sky let down its first deluge; huge droplets fell from above and began bouncing off the dusty ground. 'AWA!' yelled the king, (meaning forbidding). "Call the rain-makers! Nothing will spoil this day, not even the weather!"

There were some people in the land who were gifted with supernatural powers, and they could make the rain stop or start at will. They were referred to in Benin as *Omuamen*, meaning 'rain-stoppers'.

At the king's call, an elderly man appeared as if from nowhere, his two teenage apprentices tagging closely at his feet. His name was Obamen, and he was well known amongst the Edo, as he was the most experienced rain-maker in the land.

"Long live the King", he said calmly, prostrating as he did so. "May you live long, O King. I knew you would need my services on this day, because I sensed that the wicked ones had planned to spoil the fun you had planned. They have drawn the rain in order to disrupt the event".

The belief that rain could be invoked in this way was commonplace amongst the Edo. In such instances, a higher spiritual power would be needed to counter or subdue those of the evil-minded people who had chosen to destroy a special occasion. If all other efforts failed, Obamen would be the last hope.

CHAPTER 3

The challenge

A s THE DRUMMING resumed, this time accompanied by the melodic sound of flutes, the atmosphere became charged with supernatural energies, and many of the fighters began to convince themselves that they were invincible.

On hearing the spiritual pulse booming forth from his own drummers—a sound that was making the hairs stand erect on every inch of every human's skin—Ugowe jigged forward as if to separate himself from the crowd, and then began to dance as if possessed, taking seven steps forward and then another seven backwards, over and over again. After he had continued in this way for several minutes, an older man stepped forward. The once-white skirt and sleeveless shirt that clung to his aging body now appeared an unusual tint of brown, mottled with the stains of sweat, herbal juices, and the blood of sacrificed animals. Ragged ropes, fashioned from material torn from clothing, were bound around his wrists, biceps, ankles and head, and a multitude of coral beads hung from every part of his attire. As he made his way closer to Ugowe, the seven small bells that swung from the strings tied around his ankles tinkled, chimed, and clanged with the vibration of every step, providing an irregular background melody to the words he was now confidently chanting:

"He who touches the tail of a rattlesnake walks in the path of death; a dog that competes against the lion gets lost in the jungle; as the day never sees the night, so Ugowe can never see defeat; he who dares to challenge the champion has agreed a date with death itself". Pausing for a moment, the old man cast a lingering gaze over the crowd and then the wrestlers. "Who amongst you has been marked this day for death?" He scanned the face of each individual, daring someone to respond, but was met with silence. Everyone knew about Ugowe and his prowess. "Is there not a man amongst you that is bold enough to visit and dine with his ancestors this day?" he cried, his voice full of scorn and his dark eyes brimming with displeasure. "Do not let this great day go by without giving my King some entertainment! Have my people become that weak?" he added with a sneer, as if to provoke someone to step up to the competition.

"Enough of the boisterous display!" shouted an old man from within the crowd. A hush immediately fell amongst the onlookers, as no one dared either dispute or accept Ugowe's challenge, and every head turned to watch the man as he continued to speak out:

"When a child chooses to grow protruding teeth, the child must first consider obtaining extra-sized lips to be able to accommodate the teeth inside the mouth. He who thinks himself to be the strongest soon finds out how weak he really is amongst the strong ones. A man who boasts about his own madness soon realises that his madness is complete sanity amongst the mad men. Can a man hold air in his hands? The lion might be the king of the jungle but the lion will get run down and killed by hunters. Today, Ugowe is the hunted and he shall be trapped down like an animal. You have called for a challenge today and a challenge you will get".

On hearing these assertions the crowd began to cheer, as they knew they were in for some exciting entertainment. Even Ugowe knew better than to underestimate his challenger, as the old man's chants had not just been words—they were a form of spiritual combat, and had countered those of his own. As the flutists began to play their instruments once more, the crowd parted to allow a pathway for the tall, athletic being who was emerging from its depths. His muscles were so well chiselled that his body looked like the work of a fine sculpture, and his skin was so dark that his white eyes appeared to radiate from their sockets. His name was Asako, and he came from a small place in Benin called Evboesi, meaning 'good village'. Asako stood a mammoth six foot five inches tall, yet his great height was disguised by the pounds of muscle he carried on his frame. He had remained undisputed in every village, including his own, but until that day had declined every invitation to wrestle in Benin with the simple reply of "not yet".

"I have heard so much about you, Ugowe, and I have longed for this day", spoke Asako, his voice cold and emotionless. "I do hope that you will make it worth my while", he added, the corners of his mouth turning upwards just a little.

"Tales of you have filled my ears as well", replied Ugowe, "and I have prayed to fight someone who will at least make me break a sweat. My wish is that your strength will at least match your big words—so do not let me down", he concluded. The respect that the two men held for each other was clear; even though they had never met until now, the news of their escapades had travelled far, and people had often wondered who would be defeated when the two fighters collided. And now the puzzle was about to be solved.

"Enough talk!" interrupted the king. "The test of strength is not done by words, so let the bouts begin."

In response to this, Asako and Ugowe bowed to greet each other before kneeling down in front of the king whilst chanting, "Oba gha to okpere." The people clapped their hands in excitement, joyful sounds erupting from the mouths of some, whilst others beat on their drums or blew their flutes as the onlookers sang and danced.

A group of men and women, swathed in white materials and many different corals, moved swiftly to the front of the crowd. The women's bodies were decorated with white chalk paint, and further corals were interwoven in their plaited hair. These were the dancers—eighteen in number—and they lined up in three rows of six. As they sang and danced to the drums as if invisibly connected, the masquerades ran out from different corners of the crowd, startling the people with their rapid somersaults and multiple air jumps that defied gravity. Some believed the masquerades to be spirits rather than human beings; but others claimed them to be men who covered themselves in plenty of raffia to conceal their identities, and who became highly possessed with spirits whenever they performed, allowing them to do things that defied science. Regardless of this difference in opinion, people were always pleased to see the masquerades and their thrilling performance, and the air resonated with the sound of cheers during this splendid form of entertainment.

By the time the wrestling started, the crowd was already feverish with excitement and yet the best was still to come at the end, as was customary in Benin. In the meantime, six men in their early twenties ran forward and lined up in pairs, and then began to fight amidst the cries of each favoured name. It did not take long before one of the first two athletes lifted his opponent and slammed him to the floor, and as soon as his victim's back hit the ground the young man was embraced by his supporters, who lifted him up in celebration of his victory. The other wrestlers also provided a spectacular show for the crowd, and were adored for it.

CHAPTER 4

Asako Remembers his Past

As Asako stood waiting for the young wrestlers to finish and his own fight to start, his mind drifted to the past and the promises he had made to his beloved Eki, whose memory he would forever cherish. Such had been the strength of the couple's love, it was still talked about throughout the village of Evboesi to this day. Back then, Asako had been just seventeen years old, and Eki only fifteen. Everyone had agreed that Eki was the most beautiful girl in the village. She was so beautiful, in fact, that even the women would remark on her stunning looks. Some of the local people claimed that she was born of the river goddess Olokun—in their belief, such beauty could only be possessed by a deity. Yet her elderly parents were poor, and life was very difficult for them.

An old chief in the village had previously sold a plot of land to this old couple, and they had worked hard to turn it into a small farm.

One day, Eki's mother made her way to the chief's house to pay the agreed sum of money for the little plot, but before she could do so, she was mugged and every penny the couple owned was taken. As a result, they were left unable to make payment to the chief as agreed. Some of the villagers believed that it was chief who was responsible for the robbery—that he had sent his thugs to steal the money as he wanted Eki's parents to remain indebted to him, thereby enabling him to implement his wicked plan, but no one had been able to prove this theory.

However, he eventually made his intentions known to the old couple himself. Having received his demand for payment, Eki's parents had decided to visit the chief at his house in order to tell him that they no longer had the money, and to offer him their services instead. As soon as they entered his home, the old man and woman both fell to their knees and began to plead with him. "Have mercy on us", Eki's father had begged. "We have nothing to our names. Everything we gathered to pay for the land was stolen from us on the very same day that the money was owed. Please, we beg you to have mercy on us. Our farmland is our only resource. We could not eat without it. You have numerous lands in Evboesi and we have been told that you have to pay a lot of money for their maintenance. Kindly let us become your labourers and we will not ask for any wage, but rather a gradual reduction of our debts". As the old couple pleaded in this way, the tears rolled freely down their cheeks.

"Shut up!" the old chief shouted in fury. "Do you think I run a charity for beggars? I have no need for any more labourers—and even if I did, what gives you the honour of thinking I would wish to use you wretched riffraff?"

The old couple's sobs grew louder. "Please have mercy on us! We beg you, in god's name!" they cried in unison.

"Why should I have mercy on you?" the chief sneered.

"If not for us, at least for the sake of our only daughter", the old couple replied. "We are old, and yet she still needs to be provided for until she gets married".

On hearing these last words, the countenance of the old chief suddenly changed; as if by magic, the anger dissipated from his face and was replaced by a smile. "People say that I am wicked and evil, but they fail to see what a philanthropist I really am", he said aloud, as if to convince himself.

"Oh! You are merciful!" cried the couple, and in attempt to gain favour the old lady gushed, "We know you are, no matter what others may say".

"Shut up!" the chief interrupted, "Before I unleash my anger on you! How dare you talk when I am speaking? You wretched bastards!" As he continued to curse them, Eki's parents bowed their heads in silence, not wishing to provoke him further.

Having regained his composure, the chief was now smiling cunningly. "I will help you clear your debts on the condition that I take your daughter, Eki, as a wife", he said.

"But you already have eight wives, and your youngest child is older than our daughter", retorted Eki's father in open-mouthed disgust.

The chief's narrow eyes flashed with fury. "Silence! How dare you open your dirty mouth to talk in my presence, you dog! Poor and wretched people, are you not happy that I am doing you a favour and making you my in-laws? Anyway, I have spoken and it shall be so whether you like it or not. I do not even want my money from you anymore, but I will come to take your daughter in seven days. Guards!" he called out in anger. "Throw these bastards out of my property!" Turning back to the horrified old couple he spat, "I am not only going to make your daughter my ninth wife, I will also reclaim my plot of land from you". He began to laugh as his guards roughly bundled them away as if they were meat carcasses. "I am coming for my wife in seven days" he shouted after them gleefully, and continued to laugh out loud as if he had gone mad.

Eight days later, the chief sent his thugs to the couple's house for Eki. However, when they got there the girl could not be found. Her parents cried and pleaded with the men, explaining that their daughter was not at home, but their words fell on deaf ears. The thugs left nothing in the little hut standing, and gave the couple a beating so severe that it left the old man with a broken leg and his wife with a cracked rib. They also threatened to return the next day.

As evening fell, Eki returned home with her lover, Asako, who at the time was the youngest wrestler in the village. He had never been defeated, and was a confident young man indeed. When Eki saw her parents' condition she wept, and begged Asako to allow her to go to the old chief, whom she feared would kill her parents if she refused to comply with his demands. On hearing this request, Asako was overcome with both compassion and anger, and he decided to pay the chief a visit himself, whereupon he asked to pay the debt owed by the old couple. However, as the chief was firmly fixed on obtaining the beautiful maiden for himself, Asako's offer was declined. The chief then ordered his guards to seize the young man and lock him up in the yard as a slave. No one could ever explain exactly what had happened next, but when Asako stepped out of that compound just moments later, all of the thugs lay lifeless. Maddened with fury, the chief had then thrust forward a charm that was believed to strike dead whomever it touched, but as he lurched towards Asako, the nimble young wrestler had stepped aside, causing the chief to fall to the ground, whereupon he had bashed his head against a stone and died.

This was a tragedy for the young wrestler. He knew what the repercussion would be for killing a chief, and so, in fear for his life, he ran away. Unbeknown to him, his beloved Eki was pregnant, and she gave birth to a boy in Asako's absence. Yet the birth was a difficult one; Eki lost a lot of blood, and the old women who were acting as midwives were unable to stop the haemorrhaging. Despite their best efforts, the young mother lost her life before she had the chance to hold her son in her arms. Her heartbroken, elderly parents took care of the baby, until they too passed away.

All of the villagers were left in sorrow about what had befallen this poor family, and they wondered how Asako could have abandoned his lover in such a way. Having resolved amongst themselves never to tell

Asako that he had a son—should he ever even return—they all took an oath never to reveal the truth.

Five years later, and having regretted his decision to run away, Asako returned to the village of Evboesi. On hearing the news of Eki's death, he wept unashamedly, blaming himself despite being unaware of how she died. He was never told of his son, who had been taken away by a warrior in the village. Being childless himself, the man had seized the opportunity of adopting the small boy after the death of the grandparents.

Standing at the graveside of his beloved, Asako made a vow to always fight a good fight and to become the best wrestler ever known. He promised to name a market in memory of Eki, even though he was aware that only the king had the power to do this. His plan was to become the best wrestler in the whole of Benin, so that when the king offered him corals and wealth as a reward for his feats, he could ask for a market to be named after Eki instead. From that day onwards, he trained and fought with the utmost dexterity.

CHAPTER 5

The Clash

A S THE SOUND of the drums and the cheering from the crowd began to intensify, Asako was forced out of his reverie. Shaking his head, he tried to push the images of Eki from his mind and focus on the fight ahead. *I know I will be facing a tough opponent today, but I will impress the king. No one will prevent me from fulfilling the promises that I have made to my beloved—not even Ugowe,* Asako told himself, and he began to dance to the sound of the drums and the flutes. As he danced, his muscles began to swell as if they were feeding directly from the beats produced by the drum.

The crowd began to cheer more loudly, and as he raised his head to find out why, Asako saw that two of the young wrestlers had defeated their opponents almost immediately, and having shown their loyalty to the king, had begun to walk away. As they did so, Ugowe stepped forward. The time had come for the main event.

"My dear King, today I have a challenger from a little village, who has promised to give a good fight", Ugowe began. "May I ask that if this wrestler can defeat me on this day, I should be permitted to resign from fighting." So confident was he that no one could defeat him, he added: "May I also ask, my lord, that should this wrestler win, he be given all of the plots of land belonging to me in Benin."

"What do you have to say to that?" the king said, turning to Asako.

"O King, may you live long. I do not seek gold nor do I seek silver. All I ask is that you allow me to rename one of the markets in Benin", he responded. A murmur rippled through the crowd. Everyone had expected to hear him ask for some form of wealth. Little did they know that Asako's request had been his goal and only focus since learning of the death of his beloved.

"That is a strange thing for anyone to ask! May I inquire as to why you have made this request?" replied the king.

"My Lord, I do not seek pity nor do I seek unearned favour. I would prefer not to give my reason on this day, if that is acceptable. May you live long, my lord", Asako concluded.

"We have all seen Ugowe wrestle, and we do not know if you can defeat him. Your words suggest that your reason for this bout has nothing to do with wealth—therefore, I will grant your request if you can so much as last the first ten minutes against him", said the king. "Now let the bouts begin!" he cried, and everyone shouted, "*Iyare*".

On hearing Asako's selfless words, some of Ugowe's supporters quickly changed their favour, and soon the crowd's cheers were divided between the two wrestlers.

As both men stood facing each other, they began to chant incantations. Ugowe's lean, powerful body was already dripping with sweat, and as Asako laid his hands on his opponent in an attempt to lift him off the ground, he found that he was unable to gain any purchase. He realised instantly that Ugowe must have used a charm that had made his body slippery and therefore impossible to lift. As Asako paused, pondering over how to overcome this tactic, he felt his legs being raised from the ground. Ugowe had taken advantage of the moment, and, with his taut arms wrapped around Asako's torso, was already lifting the brave challenger into the air.

"AWA", shouted Asako, his voice urgent. "It is forbidden to lift a baby up and drop the baby on the ground", he chanted. "So whenever a baby is carried up, care is taken not to drop him".

At these words, Ugowe found that he was unable to release Asako, whose spell had taken effect the moment it had passed from his lips.

On seeing this drama unfolding before them, the crowd began to exclaim in excitement—whilst many different charms had been seen in operation, never before had this type been witnessed.

The elderly man who had thrown open Ugowe's challenge took a step forward, the bells around his ankles tinkling once more with the movement. Casting a quick glance at Ugowe, who was now sweating profusely, he could see that the strength was draining out of the fighter with every second that passed; Ugowe was weakening rapidly, his muscles palpitating from being forced into holding Asako's body in the air. The elderly man quickly started a recital; the words that spilt from his mouth were some strange form of incantation. As he chanted, the old man that had introduced Asako stepped forward and began to energise his fighter in the same way. Suddenly, Ugowe was able to move his hands again and Asako quickly jumped backwards, his agility preventing him from falling to the ground. On seeing this everyone cheered, and each person present was convinced that the two wrestlers were perfectly matched.

But when Ugowe lifted his hands and began to wave them at Asako, the crowd began to scream. Even the people at the back could see the effect of this action. Asako was staggering around as if in total darkness whilst Ugowe now walked stealthily behind him, waiting for the right moment to grab his opponent and throw him to the ground. He knew that he could not afford to approach him carelessly—a man like Asako was dangerous, even without his sight.

A shout from the old man who was supporting Asako broke through the screams. "Do not think about your sight! Forget trying to use your eyes, Asako the great; without your eyes, you remain great".

In response to this supernatural support, Asako shouted out, "A bat is born blind, yet it sees", and he immediately became aware of everything around him. As Ugowe approached once more, Asako caught hold of his arms in one swift movement, and then, wrapping his own hands around Ugowe's neck, began to squeeze tightly. Ugowe fought frantically to release Asako's grip as he was already short of air, and in his struggle he tapped his challenger's hand twice, forgetting that this was the antidote of the blindness spell he had placed on him. At that moment, Asako regained full vision and, as if by reflex, he immediately let go of Ugowe's neck.

The two old men who were accompanying the fighters both dipped their hands into the small pouches they were carrying across their chests, before withdrawing them to reveal a powdery substance. Leaning forward, they both blew this into the air in each other's direction. As soon as the powders clashed, the particles mingling and falling as one, Asako and Ugowe charged towards each other like raging bulls and began to wrestle. They both tried tirelessly to take each other down but each time Asako attacked, Ugowe's body would become as slippery as a wriggling fish plucked from a pond; and whenever Ugowe tried to lift Asako, the latter's body began to vibrate and increase in size, causing Ugowe to lose his grip.

The fight continued in this way for about three hours, with neither wrestler being able to overcome the other, and eventually dark clouds began to drift overhead causing the light to diminish.

Whilst the king and everyone else present were all enjoying the entertainment, they were reminded of the day Ugowe wrestled General Eboigbe for hours without there being a victor or a vanquished at the end.

"My lord", said one of the chiefs, turning to address the king with a wide smile. "It seems that there isn't going to be a winner today".

"I strongly disagree with you", said the king as he lifted up his right hand. "Enough!" he called out. Immediately, Ugowe and Asako stopped fighting and went down on their knees before the king, the sweat dripping freely from their steaming bodies.

"We have seen enough", the king proclaimed, "and I would say for sure that we have all been entertained. Ugowe, you remain a real man and I am honoured that you are a soldier in my army." Then, turning to face the excited crowd he called out, "You think you have not seen a victor today, but I tell you that here are two victors kneeling before me now." Stretching out his hand, he pointed to the two men who were still on their knees and declared them both to be the winners. The people cheered with jubilation, pleased with this decision as it was impossible not to like both men.

CHAPTER 6
The King makes an Offer

Turning to Asako, the king continued to speak in his authoritative tones. "You fight with so much passion. I have not seen any man fight the way you do, until today. I will grant your desires, and I ask in return that you stay in my palace as the leader of the palace guards".

The crowd jumped up in excitement, happy that the king had agreed to honour Asako the stranger whom they had come to love already. "What is your response to this?" the king asked of the courageous wrestler.

"My lord, may you live long and may you reign forever", Asako responded. "I would like to thank you for granting my request and for the honour that you have given to me by inviting me into your palace. It means so much to me and for that I owe you my life, but what would that life mean to me if there were no more fights to be had? Fighting is what I do best, and it is all I know how to do. O great one, do not take that away from me, or it would mean that I have been punished on this day".

"Shut your mouth before I order the guards to cut off your tongue!" shouted one of the palace chiefs, leaping to his feet. "Don't you know that it is a privilege to be chosen by the king to serve in the palace? It is forbidden to refuse! If the king has spoken, then so shall be it."

At this outburst, a hush fell over the people, the joyous smiles wiped from their faces and replaced by expressions of sadness. They knew Asako was treading on dangerous ground: no one ever dared to oppose the king.

Yet after a momentary hesitation, the king spoke once more, this time in a voice tinted with surprise. "I have heard you", he said, looking straight at Asako. "The gods have favoured you this day and so will I. Since you have survived your fight against Ugowe and have asked for neither gold nor silver, I will grant your request. I will also give you some precious corals and, because you love fighting, I ask that you become a soldier in my army".

"Long live the king. From this day onwards, I will serve in your army and never turn my back on this land", replied Asako as he bowed down his head before the king.

At this, Ugowe began to speak. "May you reign forever, my king. It will be a pleasure to have a man like Asako fight by my side. If it pleases you, my lord, I shall introduce him to the General at once". A smile erupted over Ugowe's proud face as he shook hands with Asako and then gave him a pat on the shoulder.

"Continue your celebration, and I will retire to my chamber", the king said as he got up from his seat.

"*Iyare*", the people shouted as they dropped to their knees. "Long live the king."

Meanwhile, in a village lying on the border of Benin, the *Ovie* (or 'ruler') was addressing his people who were assembled before him. "I greet you all", he said clearly, looking around his packed courtyard. "As you may know, we are all gathered for the same purpose. We have in our midst a white man from Britain, whom I believe might have the answer to our problems. He has requested that I summon you here today so that he can address you in person. I would appreciate it if we could all hear him out".

All eyes immediately flickered to the visitor and his comrades, who were evidently struggling with the stifling heat. Standing bare-chested, their pale skin glinting in the harsh sunlight, the three men were swatting aimlessly at the flies that were swarming around them, slapping their own bodies as each insect made contact over and over again. Being used to such conditions, the villagers had come better prepared; each held a stick from which dangled the tip of a horse's tail, and every so often they would flick these instruments to the left and then to the right of their shoulders, scattering the flies as they did so.

Whilst the rulers and representatives of other nearby villages were amongst the huge number of people gathered, they were outnumbered at least three times over by these locals, who had congregated out of sheer curiosity in the hope of getting a proper look at the foreigners.

One of the leaders of a neighbouring village turned to address the Ovie. "Since you have received the visitors and have accommodated them", he said smoothly, "I believe that they mean good, as they would not have survived in your land if they meant otherwise. Therefore, I agree to listen to what the foreign men have to say". As he looked around to gauge people's reaction to this, there were several approving nods from the other rulers present.

Three of the bare-chested British men stood up in the midst of the locals, and one of them began to speak to the gathering while a village native interpreted.

"I greet you in the name of Her Majesty the Queen", said the spokesman stiffly. "We have travelled here from afar, and are impressed with what we have seen. Her Majesty the Queen sends her greetings, and she would like to know if there is anything that you would like us to help you with: schools for your children, for example, or bridges and roads and so on. Just say the words, as we have come to help you".

Hushed whispers rippled through the small group of rulers, who were uncertain of how to respond to the visitors. Finally, after what seemed like an hour at least, one of them turned back to the British men. "*Wa do*", he said, meaning 'welcome'. "You are all welcome to our land—we greet you. First of all, I would like to say that although the interpreter was quite helpful, I found it difficult to understand a lot of your speech".

Before he could continue, another of the rulers stood up. "We do not need anything from you or your people; we are all happy with what we have", he snapped. "So go and tell your leader that we do not want anything from him."

"We have come in the name of the queen, who is our leader. All we are trying to do is to help your people by providing education, good roads, and medicine", replied the British spokesman in an attempt to reassure the villagers. "All we ask is that you hear us out and give us the opportunity to help you".

"This is too much for my ears", retorted another of the rulers. Turning to the Ovie, he asked incredulously, "You called us here to listen to people who are being ruled by a woman?"

"Enough!" shouted the Ovie. "These people have come from afar; they have not asked for anything but have offered to give our children an education and provide decent medicine. If these are their intentions then we need to show them hospitality".

The whole crowd fell silent as the rulers looked to each other hesitantly. After a long pause, everyone began to nod in agreement to the Ovie's suggestion.

Looking to the spokesman, the Ovie asked: "How powerful is this woman leader of yours?"

"Very powerful" he responded, nodding his head as if to strengthen the statement.

"If this is so", said the Ovie, "we have just one request to make. We do not require anything else from your people but this one small favour. Our only problem is this: we rely greatly on the trade between us and the people of Benin, our neighbours, and have done so for a long time. However, the king of Benin has now made a decree that prohibits us from trading with them, and this is badly affecting us as most of the things we use on a daily basis come from this place. Therefore, if your people can help us to change this decision, whatever you want from us we will do".

"Can you lead us to this king so that we can plead on your behalf straight away?" a fat British man asked casually. Immediately all of the people looked to their leader in horror, jaws gaping and eyes wide at this senseless statement.

"Haven't you heard of the Edo?" the Ovie bellowed, his brow furrowing with anger. Without waiting for a reply, he launched into a furious tirade. "Do you think you can just go into the kingdom without an invitation?" His arms were now waving wildly in the air. "For your information, these people are very powerful and they like to be treated with respect. For your own sake, I advise you to approach them with reverence if you wish to succeed with this task. We do not want the king to be angry with us for allowing you to act as our representatives."

All the other rulers began to whisper urgently amongst one another, suddenly against the decision to allow the British intervene on their behalf.

Realising that the revelation of the full extent of their plans would be most unwelcome amongst this particular gathering, the British men stood up to leave. "Thank you everyone for being so hospitable", said the spokesman with a polite nod of his head. "We have heard all that you have to say, and we assure you that we will take your request to our queen. You should hear from us shortly". With that they began to walk back towards their boat where their captain was waiting for them.

CHAPTER 7

Caution is thrown to the wind

ONCE BACK IN the sanctuary of their boat, the British men began to laugh raucously, swigging from cans of beer whilst imitating the voices of the village rulers. Music that was alien to these shores blared from a stereo, filling the air with strange notes and capturing the attention of the animals in the forest, which ceased their rustles to listen—cock-headed in bewilderment—to these foreign sounds. As the African land lay in silence, the revelry on the boat became louder; the men were laughing, drinking, and puffing their thick cigar smoke into the clear air.

"What should we do?" shouted one of them to their captain. "Should we go and visit the so-called 'Benin king' in the morning?" His voice was full of ridicule, and all of the men burst out laughing once more, some slapping their comrade on the back.

The captain, however, remained serious. "Now that you have asked, I will tell you. We could go back to England and get more support, or we could arrange a meeting with the king. I am sure he would receive us in the name of the Queen, but we must not be foolish by disregarding the advice given by the locals".

These words were met by jeers and sneers of contempt from several of the men. The captain stood to face them, his mouth taut with anger. "We have no right over this kingdom" he said, having raised his voice considerably.

Startled by this unexpected response the men fell instantly silent and their eyes dropped to the floor. Taking in the expressions of shock, the captain regained his composure and began to speak in his usual calm manner. "The king is not stupid", he said as if to explain his outburst. "A few years back, I was part of the team that visited Benin. It was surprising to see such an advanced kingdom in Africa. We saw real wealth in that land, and since then we have been doing everything we can to get the king to sign a treaty. We want it to become a British colony, but that stubborn king has completely refused our wishes".

"What we should do is disguise the contract that he needs to sign. I bet he can't even read—he'll sign it!" said one of the men confidently.

"We have tried that before", replied the captain. "We told him that it was an agreement for friendship and trade with the British but he was wise enough to smell a rat; since then, he has banned all British officials and traders from entering his kingdom. So now we are looking for a means to remove him from the throne so that we can have access into the land as we please. Discussions are still ongoing, as making this kingdom a British colony will be very costly; however, I believe that just the riches from the king's palace alone would be enough to cover the costs". He stared up at the dark sky for a minute before turning back to point at one of the men who was still slurping from a beer can. "Write a letter to the king immediately", he ordered, his tone sharp. "Inform him of our impending arrival". Turning to the others, he smiled. "This way, we will have shown the desired respect by notifying them of our intended visit".

"But you said there is an imposed ban on all British nationals that prohibits them from entering the land!" slurred the man in alarm. "How do you plan to get around that?"

"And why did you say that the king would receive us in the name of the Queen?" chipped in another.

The captain laughed quietly, and leaning forward removed the beer can from the drunken man's hand. Tilting his head back, he poured the remains into his mouth before crushing the empty can in his hand and throwing it out to sea. "Because", he said, smacking his lips together as he spoke, "the name of the Queen opens doors everywhere—even in Africa".

At this, the men began stumbling around on the deck in guffaws of laughter, and one raised his right hand like a petulant schoolboy. "Can I ask a question?" he said, confusion shadowing his face.

The group fell silent once more.

"Yes", they all chorused, their attention now focused on this one man.

"Captain, you have said we should write to those primitive, uneducated people, but you have forgotten to say in what language we should write the letter in," he said, his eyes wide with false innocence and his hand still stretched up into the air. They all fell about laughing once again.

"Can you believe it . . . those backward people were ridiculing the idea of a female ruler! I have never heard of people that are more foolish or uncivilised", interrupted another.

"I would love to go and wipe out all those animals, and take over their land and all that is in it were it not for the political implication! We need to put our flag on this kingdom!" cried a third.

The men continued in this way throughout the night, as each of them had something funny to say about the locals they had visited.

CHAPTER 8

The arrival of a strange lad

"**B**RING THE BOY to me", said the king to one of the servants.

"Here he is", came the instant reply, as a child was nudged forward and encouraged to kneel.

"What brings you here?" the king asked, looking down at this unexpected visitor who was now on his knees before him.

"I am Osaro, the son of the greatest warrior from the village of Evboesi", the boy declared, brimming with confidence. "Just before my father died he told me to come to Benin, as it is my destiny to protect the king."

Everyone began to laugh at this boy who was claiming to be destined to protect the greatest king ever.

"Quiet!" one of the chiefs shouted down at the child. "Don't you know that words like that will get you killed? What is your father's name?" he demanded.

"That is enough!" interrupted the king. "If he believes his destiny is to protect me then I would prefer it to be so than for it to be otherwise". He smiled down at the innocent-looking boy, having taken an immediate shine to him. "What did you say your name was again?" he asked, this time taking a closer look at the subject before him. The boy could be no more than sixteen years old, was very dark in complexion, and stood at around five feet eight inches tall. He was wearing brown khaki shorts and a small, brown cotton shirt that had evidently seen better days: the material was faded and three of the front buttons were missing. At his side was a large bag containing an old machete and a bow with many arrows, all of which had been made by himself. A few clothes that were stuffed in the bottom were in no better condition than the ones that hung from his lean body.

As if writing on an unseen object, the king began to draw an invisible sign in the air with his index finger. Then, with brightened eyes, he began to speak. "I am taking more of an interest in your village now, as not too long ago a wrestler came from there and gave a very good fight. We all saw his performance, didn't we?" he asked, turning to the chiefs and servants that were present.

"Yes, my lord, we all witnessed it", they replied, their voices betraying the confusion they were feeling. They could not understand the reason for the king's reference to the great warrior, Asako, who had indeed put up a remarkable performance not so long ago.

"I do believe that good things come from Evboesi village, and because of Asako, who is now one of my soldiers, I will favour anyone who comes from there", the king said, as if reading their minds. "Are you a warrior or a wrestler?" he asked, looking back to the young lad who was now looking around the palace with admiration.

The boy cleared his throat. "I am neither a warrior nor a wrestler but one destined to protect his king", he replied with a confidence that seemed out of keeping with his innocent looks.

"But how are you going to protect the king if you can't even protect yourself?" the chief asked mockingly.

"Easy on the boy", said the king. "My instinct tells me that I can trust him. Therefore, I will personally keep a close eye on him. In order for me to be able to do this I will make him my *Omuada*". In Benin, this title was given to the staff bearer whose duty it was to stand at the side of the king.

"It is clear now what the boy is destined for", sneered another of the chiefs. "He has been destined to carry the sword of the king!" All those gathered began to chuckle.

"You may all go about your various businesses now. I will spend time with Osaro and find out more about him", the king retorted coldly.

"Long live the king. You are in good hands! So we will take our leave now". As the men walked away, talking amongst each other about the young lad and his acclaimed destiny, their laughter could still be heard from inside the palace.

A few weeks later, the king called a meeting with the chiefs and elders of the land.

"Long live the king", the chiefs chorused as they gathered before him.

"Thank you, my people", he said with a brisk nod. "I have summoned you today as I sense that something bad is about to happen. My staff bearer, Osaro, whom you all know, had a dream that keeps on repeating itself. He has also informed me that his dreams never go unfulfilled. The reason I have called you is to ask you to sit down and check yourselves; if there is anything that may cause anger in this land, I want you all to sort it out now".

"May you live long, my king", said one of the chiefs. "Was this not the same boy who claimed that he was destined to protect you? I have had my doubts concerning that child from the very first day I set eyes on him", he continued. "And I wouldn't be surprised if he was sent to sow fear in the hearts of our people, so that we may be weakened in the event of an attack". The chief paused as if to consider his next words with care. "My lord", he began again, this time with a note of caution in his speech. "He is such a strange child. We advised that the oracle be consulted in order to learn of his intentions, but you ruled against it. We know your instinct is never wrong, my lord, and as your subjects we will support whatever you say". The chief's intention towards diplomacy was startlingly evident; he knew too well that any suggestion implying the king to be wrong could cost him his own head. "I do not think we should be worried about his silly dreams, or bother to waste the time of the chief priest with these matters".As he finished speaking, the palace courtyard echoed with the murmurs and hisses that were coming from the mouths of the other chiefs, none of whom liked Osaro and his ridiculous claims of protecting the king. The fact that the king had become so fond of the boy, treating him differently to the other servants, had strengthened their dislike even more.

"If he is seeing bloodbaths in his dreams, he may be correct", said another chief who had been standing quietly. "We are Edo; we are warriors; and we do not lose any battle. This is why we are feared by all. Look around", he said, standing up from his seat and making a sweeping gesture."Is there any village that would dare to challenge us to a battle? Besides, as my lord has decreed, this is a time for peace and we have made all the villages aware of this. They have all been pleased to hear that as well, so if any of them decide to touch the tail of a rattlesnake just because the head is looking away, then they should be prepared for the repercussion".The chief's breath was now coming more rapidly, and so he paused for air before concluding. "All I am saying is this: Osaro's dream may mean that some villages are preparing to wage war against us, and we will make them swim in their own blood". As he retook his seat the other chiefs nodded their heads in agreement, reassured by this interpretation.

"Our soldiers have been getting bored as there have been no battles to fight", added one of the elders."So whoever decides to be the unlucky one by waging war will pay dearly for it."

Taking in the further nod of heads amongst the men, the king spoke once again. "Let all of us tread carefully for the next three months, until the dark clouds that I am sensing now have passed away", he instructed.

"Long live the king", was the reply, and the meeting was drawn to an end.

CHAPTER 9
A Difficult Message

OST OF THE chiefs and elders had already left the palace when the chief priest of the land entered the courtyard singing the praises of the king. In his late fifties, this man knew how to walk with confidence, and the bells that were tied around each of his legs clanged with every long stride, merrily announcing his arrival. In his hand was a walking stick made of iron, from which hung a multitude of charms, and it was clear that its purpose was not to support the man's weight. The same stick had been held by his fore-fathers, and had been passed on through the generations—for it was believed that anyone visiting the shrine of the gods without it would be struck dead.

Those who remained in the palace courtyard were all scared to see the priest, as he only appeared when the gods wished to give a warning to the land or a particular instruction to the king.

What is he doing here? was the only thought running through people's minds as the priest came to a standstill in front of the throne.

"Long may you live, my king." His voice was loud and echoed authority. "I sense a dark cloud, my lord, and I have been sent by the gods to inform you of this immediately."

"This is so strange", replied the king. "I have felt the same thing, and my *omuada* keeps dreaming of a bloodbath, but the elders think it is nothing. What have the gods asked for this time?" he asked, a hint of uncertainty creeping into his normally austere voice. He knew only too well that to ignore any warning from the gods would be detrimental. "Tell me", he demanded. "Should I sacrifice a goat? A cow? Just name it!"

"The gods have not demanded any sacrifice, my lord", returned the priest. "They say that this is a choice that you will have to make as a king. If you choose right, all shall be well; but if you choose incorrectly, then the land shall be covered in blood."

"You speak in parables", said the king impatiently. "I need to know what I must do! Have the gods decided to leave me in darkness?" he finished, hoping for a better answer.

"What the gods have instructed me to do I have done, my lord, but I will tell you this. Avoid spilling any blood on this land for at least three months after the festive period, and in that way you will pass whatever test this is. Long may you live, my king. I have done what I have been instructed to do. Now it is up to you, my lord, to do your own part."

As he was about to leave, the priest's gaze fell upon young Osaro who was standing by the king, and his authoritative tone filled the courtyard once more. "Great Osaro! A man destined for greatness; children yet unborn will hear about you and your deeds. For you to achieve this, you must let old secrets remain secrets." Having issued this strange warning, the priest looked back to the king. "You have made the right decision to keep him here with you", he concluded. Facing away from the door and with his eyes still firmly fixed on the king, the priest began to move backwards, and after about seven steps he raised his stick up high, before bringing it crashing to the ground. As the harsh sound of metal upon stone reverberated around the walls of the courtyard, the old man vanished into thin air.

Whilst the king and everyone else present were surprised at the priest's words about Osaro, it was the warning of bloodshed that was uppermost in their minds. For this reason, little thought was given to the fact that the priest knew Osaro by name despite having never met him before, and no one mulled over the priest's statement that children yet unborn would remember Osaro's deeds. *Maybe he will be an exceptional servant of the king and be remembered for that,* one of the chiefs thought simply in passing.

The news from the priest had made the king even more worried, and questions were running through his mind. *What test could this be, and why was the chief priest not allowed to tell me more? Why have the gods not asked for any sacrifice?* The harder he thought the more anxious he became, later that evening he sent for Osaro in an attempt to gather more clues.

"Osaro, you know that I have been very good to you since the day that you entered this land. Was there anything else in your dreams that you think I should know about?" probed the king. "Kindly tell me, and do not be afraid."

"My lord", said Osaro, who was fearful for the king as he had formed a strong bond with him already. "I have told you everything that I saw. The dreams are always the same, and start and finish at the same point. If I knew about anything else I would have told you, as I cannot hide anything from you my lord", he added. "Whatever be the case, I will have to die before anything evil happens to you".

On hearing these words the king felt his heart lift. "That is the statement that causes the chiefs to be offended", he said, unable to hide his smile. "You know that I am a warrior and can defend myself, and besides, I have great fighters all over the land that are willing to put down their lives for me. You are a young boy and have not seen much of life—and you are neither a fighter nor a warrior, so how can you protect me?" he asked as he looked at Osaro lovingly.

"I have got a machete and a bow with lots of arrows that were given to me by my late father and I can make more arrows by myself", the boy replied in his innocent voice. "With these I will protect you, my lord".

"It pleases me to hear this, but it takes more than a machete, bow and arrow to fight a battle", the king chortled. "Nevertheless, let us pray that the day when I will have to depend on you to save me will never come." He smiled at the young boy before turning around and walking alone into his inner chamber where his wives lay sleeping.

CHAPTER 10
A Letter is Received

THREE DAYS HAD passed since the chief priest visited the palace and gave the disturbing message from the gods to the king. Although these words were still clear in everyone's mind, they had all continued with their daily affairs, and today the palace was full of villagers, chiefs, and elders. The king was seated on his throne as he presided over a land dispute between two families. This was usual practise in Benin; disputes that could not be settled amicably were brought to the palace so that the king could intervene, and his verdict would always be final as his opinion was believed to be just.

Suddenly, there was a loud noise and everyone turned to see a messenger of the palace running into their midst.

"My lord! My lord!" he was shouting, seemingly unbothered about interrupting the ongoing meeting. "There is a message for you, my great king, and it is from the foreigners!"

"What is the message?" asked one of the chiefs, who had jumped up in anger of having such an important discussion disturbed.

"Here it is", the messenger replied, thrusting a sheet of paper towards the chief, who took it and then attempted to hand it over to the king.

"Read it out", objected the king, stretching out his hands as if to warn him not to come any closer with the paper.

"My Lord, it says here that the white men are coming to visit this land, having been sent by their queen. They also say that there is a matter which they would like to discuss with you," the chief read, his eyes scanning the note rapidly.

"When do they say they are coming?" the king asked, his brow furrowing.

"In two weeks time, my lord".

The king bowed his head momentarily, and then jerked it up and began to issue his commands. "You must write to the white men at once. Tell them that they have not been invited into our land; remind them that they came once before and even though we received them warmly, they decided to pay us with lies, deceit, and deception. For that reason, they are no longer welcome here. Let them know that this is our festivity period and as such, we would like all visitors to stay away", he finished.

"I will do so at once", responded the chief.

The British men were drinking and puffing smoke rings into the air when the messenger delivered the letter from the king. On reading it, the captain was infuriated.

"What nonsense!" he shouted, waving the letter round as if it was burning his fingertips. "How dare these uncivilised people refuse us entry into their heathen kingdom despite being told that Her Majesty the Queen has approved of this visit?"

"No wonder those villagers whom we visited first said that the Edo are proud people", said one of the men.

"I think they are very arrogant", spat another.

"I quite agree", added a third, nodding vigorously.

The captain held up his hand. "Tomorrow, we will go and see this stubborn, so-called king. We will ignore his disgusting words and visit anyway. What can those primitive people do to us? We have not come to fight them, so tomorrow they will have to listen to what we have to say". Turning on his heel, he stalked away from his men, who were now casting doubtful glances at each other. They were not so sure if they agreed with their captain's decision to visit the Benin king, but they were certainly not going to oppose him.

CHAPTER 11
The Regrettable Action

THE NEXT MORNING the Benin elders and chiefs had gathered once more, and with the customary greetings over, all faces were eagerly turned towards the king, who now began to address his people whilst sitting on his splendid throne. Osaro stood firmly by his side, holding the staff upright.

"My good people", boomed the baritone voice. "Last night I had a dream that some of you did something to provoke the anger of the gods. And so I am telling you all now: let everyone check themselves and get rid of anything in their possession that is unclean. No evil deeds shall be done in this land; otherwise, the consequences will be severe".

"Long may you live", the people responded. Suddenly, the beating of drums began to resound through the palace and as the rumbling continued, everyone began to crane their necks in an attempt to see what was going on, whispering to one to another as they did so. All of them knew that this was a tune played only to signal the arrival of visitors to the land.

Walking towards the palace with the escort of a few soldiers from the Benin army, the British men were looking around in admiration, oblivious to the stares that met them as they passed. "This place is different to the others we have visited", the captain whispered to his men as they entered the palace. "These people are far more civilised; this would be an excellent place to put up the British flag".

"Don't allow them into the courtyard!" yelled one of the chiefs in alarm. "They will defile our land."

"Let them remain in the outer courts!" another shouted to the soldiers.

The king stood up, his expression grave, and quietly ordered the white men to be taken to a different yard where important guests were usually received.

"We come in the name of Her Majesty", yelled one of the foreigners over his shoulder.

"Be quiet!" a chief shouted over him. "How dare you speak before the king?"

"Unfortunately, we will not be able to give you the type of reception that we would normally give to our visitors". The king towered above the foreigners now standing before him. "I did send word to inform you that you are not welcome here. Your people have been dishonest and tried to steal from us in the past. Did you not get this message?"

The British captain met the king's stony glare without flinching. "Yes, we did", his voice matter of fact. "But we thought that, since we would not be taking too much of your time, we might as well come to see you. We want you to reconsider your stance about trading with us—and with your neighbours as well".

At this response, the king felt his nostrils beginning to flare and he struggled to maintain his composure. "You will have to go away immediately", he ordered. "My words are final. I will let you go in peace but you must not return, otherwise you will be asking for trouble. Whatever you have come to say must have been worth taking such a great risk for, but I will send some of my chiefs to accompany you to your boats, and you will be blindfolded as they escort you out of this land. This is just customary, you understand, especially as it is our festival period. We wouldn't like to expose our secret to visitors, which is part of the reason for my refusal of your visit—not forgetting also, of course, that your people tried to steal from my kingdom".

Despite his disappointment in the foreigners' behaviour, the king, as gracious and polite as ever, presented the British men with some gifts in order to compensate them for the inconvenience. He then sent them back to their boats with chiefs and palace guards as escorts.

As the line of men departed for the shore, total silence accompanied them. Finally, when one chief could bear it no more, he spoke up. "These stupid people! They dare to disrespect our king; even though they were told not to visit, they refused to listen. I don't know why the king showed them mercy".

"I agree with you", nodded one of his comrades. "I think they should be punished, for anyone who disrespects our king should be taught a lesson".

"Why don't we just kill them here in the forest?" asked a third chief, carefully looking for the consent of the others.

It did not take much to persuade them, however, as they were all confident that no one would find out about their actions. And so the guards were ordered to carry out the deed with their machetes, and as they did so, the British men screamed in agony and shouted out for help. But their cries only went as far as the wind could carry them across the forest, before fading out amongst the sound of the birds singing in the trees. Five minutes later, the men lay dead, each in a pool of his own blood.

As the chiefs headed back towards the palace, they made a pact to keep what had happened as a secret. Little did they know that two of the foreigners were still alive, although very badly wounded. Somehow, these men managed to get back to their boat where their comrades were waiting. Once the injured were aboard, the boat engines were started, and then the purring grew distant as the vessel disappeared into the inky night.

Three months later, the king of Benin received a letter from England. It stated that the killing of messengers who had been sent by the Queen on a peaceful mission was a declaration of war, and therefore the British now promised to erase Benin from the map.

On reading this, the king summoned the chiefs who had been ordered to escort the visitors to the shore.

"What have you done?" he roared. "You killed the men that should have been taken to their boat, and as a result their people have declared war against us!" His eyes were aflame with anger. "You know that disobeying my command will cost you dearly, but for now there are more pressing matters to worry about".

"My king", pleaded one of the chiefs responsible. "Those men disrespected your orders! You instructed them not to visit, but they ignored your message and still came. I say that they deserved what they got. Let them come! We will teach them the true meaning of battle." The others present all nodded to confirm their support.

"Enough of this rubbish!" shouted the king. "If death was the correct punishment for those foreigners that disobeyed me, what should happen to the chiefs who did the same?"

This question was met by silence, as all the men knew better than to aggravate the king even more, especially as he was now pacing up and down.

"Send for Eboigbe at once!" he barked, and a servant ran off to fetch the General before the king had even finished speaking.

Five minutes later, General Eboigbe dropped to his knees. "My lord, you summoned me", he said. He had been serving in the Benin army for almost twelve years, and was renowned for his fierceness in battle. He had led the army into several wars and each time had returned victorious. Short but exceedingly solid, Eboigbe exhibited the broadest of chests from which enormous muscles bulged as if they were trying to escape his stout frame. His taut skin gleamed in the sunlight, coating his body in the richest of chocolate right up to the top of the shaved skull that added to the ferociousness of his appearance. Charms hung all over his naked torso, and he carried the head of a leopard given to him by the king, which signified authority and the power to dominate or take life if necessary. From his broad hips hung a red skirt that was encrusted with coral beads and cowries, and, as usual, he carried a huge machete that featured the widest of blades, the handle of which was hidden within the depths of one of his massive, balled fists.

"It is not good news", said the king, "especially at a time like this when we are supposed to be celebrating". He then summarised the event that had taken place with the chiefs and the visitors, before finally informing the General of the resulting threat from the British.

"My lord", said the General as the king reached his conclusion. "In as much as I personally disagree with the chiefs' actions, particularly as you had instructed otherwise, I would say now that there is no time for regrets. Instead, we need to prepare for war. I will take my men and guard the borders of this land. I swear by my life that the British will not be able to penetrate the blockades and barriers that my men and I will erect".

"Very well", said the king. "You may go now and prepare your men."

"Thank you, my lord. Long may you live", Eboigbe replied, and disappeared from the palace.

CHAPTER 12

Search for the Army General

L ATER THAT EVENING when the king was alone in the courtyard, Osaro confidently made his approach. "My lord, may you live long. I have a favour to ask of you", he said, looking as innocent as ever.

"Go on, Osaro, you know I will do anything for you provided it is not a silly request", the king responded.

"No my king, this is not a silly request. I have been thinking of joining the army" he said, his voice shaking in anticipation of the response.

The king looked at him and began to laugh, and when he had finished laughing he spoke with a twinkle in his eye. "Oh little boy! A child can never tell how far a journey is if he or she is being carried on the mother's back. No matter how tall a boy is, he cannot see as far off as an old man".

"My lord, forgive my ignorance, your parable is strange to me and I do not understand any of it".

"That is my point", the king cut in. "I will make this easy for you. You are a little boy, and it takes a man to be a soldier—and I am not referring to age. I will permit you to discuss this with the General; if you can convince him to accept you into the army then I might consider releasing you of your present duty." With that, he walked away from the open area of the courtyard and into his chambers.

On hearing the king's words, Osaro sprinted out of the palace yard and onto the street in search of the General. The village was buzzing with people going about their daily affairs: traders were standing by their stalls, calling out their wares at the top of their voices; boys and girls were street hawking, balancing trays laden with fruits and other foods on their heads; locals were zigzagging from one stall to another, bartering with the vendors in high-pitched voices in an attempt to be heard above the hubbub.

Unsure of where he was heading, Osaro was frantically looking from left to right as he ran, veering in and out of the chaos in the hope of catching sight of a soldier who could point him in the direction of Eboigbe. Suddenly, as if out of nowhere, a young girl appeared in his path, a tray piled with oranges carefully balanced on her head. Despite his attempts to swerve around her, Osaro felt the breath whoosh out of his lungs and an almighty clatter filled his ears. The girl had instinctively released her hold on the tray so that she might break her fall with her hands, and now a multitude of bright oranges were tumbling all around, bouncing to the ground in rapid succession, some pelting her legs as she lay sprawled on the ground, the tray resting upside down on her stomach. Osaro quickly fell to his knees and began grappling around on the dusty surface of the street, desperately trying to capture the oranges as they rolled underneath the feet of those passing by.

"I am so sorry", he gasped, taking the tray from the girl's belly and carefully arranging the dirty, battered-looking fruit back in its original pattern. He cast a despairing look after those that were merrily trundling into the distance before turning back to the girl, who was now speaking in the softest of voices.

"It is okay, I am also to blame", she was saying, a shy smile forming as she spoke. "If I had reacted more quickly I could have avoided you".

Although the girl was still in mid-speech, Osaro was no longer hearing the words that fell from her mesmerising lips, so overcome was he by her beauty. When she spoke, her teeth shone with a whiteness of the purest snow, their brightness equalled only by the light that gleamed from her dazzling eyes, which lay under the frame of smooth, arched eyebrows the colour of ebony. Her sharp features led down to the most delicately curved neck, and her hair was skilfully plaited backwards in tiny weaves that rose to the top of her head, giving her the appearance of being taller than she actually was. Yet although she was petite in stature, the soft curve of her hips and breasts accentuated her femininity. She was a beautiful girl—no one could dispute this fact.

"As a matter of interest, may I know why you are in so much of a hurry?" She was still smiling at him, her pretty head cocked to one side as she waited for an answer.

Osaro took a huge breath and held it for a second or two before quietly exhaling. "It is a long story", he said, hearing the strange quiver in his voice. "But since you have asked, I will summarise it. I live in the palace and work as the king's armoured bearer—but this is not enough for me. I know that I am destined to do more for the king and so I want to join the army, but no one thinks that I am good enough. I am looking for the General so that I may convince him I have what it takes to become a soldier". As he finished speaking, he flexed his chest muscles as if to convince her of his strength.

The girl's smile, however, had already faded. "Don't you know it is forbidden for the king's armoured bearer to leave the palace?" she asked, her brow crinkling with worry.

"Yes I know, but I have special permission from the king", he answered calmly, trying to reassure her.

"The king must really like you to have allowed you to go outside of his palace", she smiled.

Humbled, Osaro just stared back at her in admiration.

"So, what is your name?" she asked, breaking the silence. "I want to be able to claim the honour of knowing you when you become a soldier". The tone of sarcasm in her voice was unmistakable.

"Oh!" Osaro's eyes narrowed as he tried to conceal his disappointment at her tone. "So you do not believe that I can become a soldier?"

He was not expecting an answer but the girl quickly realised that he had misinterpreted her intended humour. "No, I do believe in you, but if you go on like this then you might never become one", she replied, her eyes twinkling. As her lips parted into a wide smile, Osaro was further taken aback by her beauty, but managed to compose himself enough to answer.

"And how do you propose that I attain my goal?" he retorted, somewhat perplexed.

"Sometimes, it is easier when men discuss such matters as this. You should speak to your father so that he can talk to whoever is in charge. They would be more likely to listen to him". She smiled again, this time in pleasure at finding a solution to the problem.

Asaro felt his head and shoulders sag as if an invisible load had crushed him from above. "This is not possible for me", he whispered. "My father passed away, and I am not from around here—I am from a little village called Evboesi—so I do not have anyone who could speak on my behalf."

"Evboesi? Interesting!" the girl exclaimed, smiling once again.

Osaro could not hide his confusion at this unexpected response. "What is so interesting about that?" His tone hinted at irritability.

"I am also from Evboesi", the girl replied, her eyes glistening with happiness to have met someone from the same village. "So, who was your father?"

"He was the greatest warrior, and known as Ogidigan".

Instantly, the girl's countenance changed and she whisked around as if to leave.

"What is the matter? Where are you going?" Osaro cried out before he could stop himself.

"You do not understand!" she cried. "And I cannot explain it to make it easier for you". As she turned back to meet his gaze, he saw that her face had lost its smile although it still retained its beauty.

"Now you make me too curious", he said. "And I hate being curious. Whatever it is, please tell me. I can help." He placed his hand on her shoulder in an attempt to reassure her.

"I cannot tell you, as everyone was forced to swear secrecy. If I tell you then I will remain an unmarried woman—the gods will see to this if I make the mistake of breaking the promise that was made in Evboesi".

As Osaro watched the tears springing from the girl's dark eyes he was moved with compassion, and he realised that he had fallen in love with this stranger. "Tell me your name", he demanded.

"My parents named me Oghogho, which means laughter—it is believed that wherever I am, there will always be laughter", she explained.

"You have truly brought laughter into my life today", said Osaro quietly, and they stood facing each other in silence.

Oghogho was the first to break the trance. "Go back to the palace", she begged. "Forget about the Army! Leave the protection of the king to the soldiers."

Osaro's face fell with dismay. "Those words hurt me so much. I have just explained to you that this is my destiny!"

"I know that you think it is your destiny, but I also know that you can choose to walk either that path or a different one. The one you are choosing will cause nothing but heartache".

Osaro looked at the maiden in astonishment, his curiosity aroused even more. "Something tells me that you know more than you are letting on. Please, I beg you! Kindly tell me what you know."

Torn between compassion and self-preservation, Oghogho stood in silence for what felt like an eternity, chewing her lower lip until it became angry and sore. "Okay", she said suddenly. "Meet me here in seven days."

"Very well then, I shall see you in seven days from now." Taking her hand in his, Osaro looked into her eyes. "Please don't lie to me. Be here in seven days time."

"I will see you soon, my hero", she replied, wriggling her hand free of his. Balancing the tray of oranges on her head once more, she began to walk away.

Osaro felt a sense of urgency wash over him, and he called after her. "Can we meet again tomorrow?" The words came out far faster than he had intended. "I promise not to ask you about any secret within the seven days! I just really want to see you again if you don't mind!"

Oghogho glanced over her shoulder, her eyes locking onto his. "I don't mind. I would be glad to meet with you again tomorrow, but only if we make it more discreet". She smoothed down her tight plaits with her free hand before continuing. "The palace chiefs might see you, and I would not be happy if you were punished for leaving the palace." Then, with a final smile, she continued on her way.

CHAPTER 13

The Truth is Uncovered

FROM THAT DAY onwards, Osaro and Oghogho met in secret. They spoke little, preferring to spend time in each other's arms, letting their hearts do the talking. The seventh day arrived so fast that neither of them realised it—until they began to talk about the day they met. Both then became conscious that today was the day when Oghogho should fulfil her promise, and although the girl was still uncertain as to whether she should reveal the secret to Osaro, she could not refuse her newly-found lover anything, and so she gave in to his dangerous demand. With her voice filled with sorrow, she looked into his eyes as she spoke. "What I am about to tell you has been a secret for years, and it may be hard for you to believe what I say. But, considering the price that I am about to pay by revealing this secret, I do hope that you will be convinced of the truth".

Osaro listened carefully as she spoke, and made up his mind then and there to believe every word that came from her mouth.

With tears welling up in her eyes, Oghogho began the tale. "The warrior Ogidigan was not your real father".

Before she could continue, Osaro burst out laughing. "Tell me this is a joke."

"I am afraid it is the truth. I understand how upsetting this may be for you", she replied nervously.

"Then who is my real father?" There was an angry edge to his voice.

"Don't worry, I will explain", answered Oghogho. "Your real father is Asako the wrestler. He loved your late mother so much. No one could understand why he deserted her when she needed him the most".

Osaro listened without speaking as she told the whole story: how his mother had died giving birth to him; how Ogidigan became his guardian; and then how he ended up adopting Osaro as his own child as he could not have any children of his own. Tears filled Osaro's eyes as he realised that the man he had grown to love as his father, whose memories he had idolised, was just a stranger who had come to his rescue when he was a baby. "Do you mean Asako—the man who wrestled against Ugowe some time ago—is my real father?" he asked finally, unable to imagine the possibility of this strange story being correct.

"Yes, he is your real father", Oghogho whispered.

Osaro fell quiet for a while, as if to allow the news to sink into his mind.

Suddenly he jumped up. "I must rush to the king at once, and let him know what you have just told me", he said excitedly, his eyes full of new hope. With his real father as a former wrestler and now a soldier in the army, and his adoptive father a renowned warrior, Osaro had a new identity. *This should help me get into the army!* he thought elatedly.

Oghogho's plaintive voice cut into the thoughts now whirling around in his mind. "You must promise to let this remain a secret between the two of us, Osaro! Revealing the truth will break Asako's heart. Imagine not knowing that you have had a son for all these years. He is very happy as a fighter, yet such news could make him change his mind!"

Osaro stopped in his tracks and looked up at Oghogho. "That would be disastrous at a time like this when the king needs him so much". His dejection was audible.

Oghogho hung her head, overcome with despair. "Now that I have told you the truth, the curse will have been activated. No one will want to marry me now!" Incapable of hiding her emotions any longer, she failed in stopping the tears escaping from her huge eyes, and one by one they rolled down her cheeks, building in momentum, and her breath now came in rasping sobs.

Barely unable to watch the young girl suffer such distress, Osaro was stabbed with remorse for making her break such a serious vow; but at the same time he was struggling to understand how the villagers could have reached such a wicked decision. The thought of Asako being unaware of the fact he had a son disturbed the boy greatly, and his mind was spinning in confusion as he grappled to pinpoint the correct course of action from here. Suddenly the words of the old chief priest started to reverberate inside his head. "Let secrets remain secrets", he whispered to himself, repeating the caution he had been given that day in the palace.

Putting his arms around Oghogho he said comfortingly, "The gods are not always right. Sometimes they get it all wrong. There is no way that you will remain unmarried, because as soon as I finish my service at the palace I will come and take you as my wife."

As she fell into his strong embrace the young girl whispered back, "That is so sweet to hear, but the gods are never wrong."

They remained silent in each other's arms for the rest of the night.

CHAPTER 14

The Invasion

AS DAWN BROKE, the tranquillity of the night was replaced with scenes of chaos. The atmosphere was charged with panic; people were running backwards and forwards and yet in no particular direction, and terrified shouts of "Fire! Fire!" could be heard over and over again.

Suddenly the warning cries were smothered by the booming and crashing echo of what sounded like thunder—only it was too close, and the ground was vibrating as if from the force of an earthquake whilst thick plumes of smoke infiltrated the air.

"My lord! My lord!" shouted a couple of chiefs as they rushed into the palace courtyard as if being chased by elephants.

"What's the matter?" cried the king in alarm. "What is the reason for all this commotion that I am hearing?"

"The white men have launched an attack on us!" yelled one of the chiefs hysterically. "They are killing everyone! Everyone, my lord!" The rest were just nodding frantically in confirmation of this statement, quite literally too scared for words.

"What about General Eboigbe and his soldiers? Are they not protecting our kingdom?" the king asked, trying to remain calm.

"I am afraid, my lord, the white men are fighting like cowards. They are standing far away using strange weapons that can reach a long distance. Our men cannot really do much whilst being attacked in this way", responded another of the chiefs, wringing his hands in ill-disguised fear. "But we are going now to assist . . . this is everyone's fight".

With that, they rushed out of sight. But instead of going to join the soldiers they fled back to their families, whereupon they hid themselves, abandoning their king.

At the entrance to Benin, General Eboigbe and his men had built barricades in an attempt to prevent the British invaders from entering the land. Now the General was gathering his soldiers together as he could see that they were in need of encouragement. They had never fought in any battles that were not face to face, and their enemy's weapons were far more sophisticated than any they had encountered before. And so standing proudly in front of his men, holding a machete above his head, the magnificent warrior began his address:

"We are Edo: We do not fear battle, nor do we run away from it. Fighting is what we do! Let us show the white men what we are made of! They may have come here with their strange weapons, and they may have promised to wipe us off the map in one day, but we will defeat them with our machetes and arrows because we fight for nothing but our land, our future, our children, and our king. Most of all, we fight for the Benin Kingdom! Today, for every one of us that dies, let five foreigners be found lying dead at their sides. Long live the king!"

At this, the soldiers responded so vehemently it was as if they had been injected with strength and courage, and drained of all fear. "Long live the king!" came the roar as they charged valiantly into battle.

From that moment Eboigbe's men fought gallantly against their attackers, matching them in terms of fatalities. The British soldiers had never seen anything like it before. As they witnessed more and more of their men falling at the hands of the Edo, they could not understand how these people were able to fight so bravely to their deaths and show no trace of fear.

"We must do something about this immediately", said the captain of the British army. "I can't afford to be losing my men to these heathens. We must change our tactics." Turning away from the scene of the battle, he instructed some of the soldiers to follow him whilst the others were left to continue fighting the natives.

This small group rushed to the neighbouring village, whereupon the captain demanded to speak the Ovie. News of the attack on the Benin kingdom had already spread around the surrounding areas, and accordingly the inhabitants were disturbed at the sight of the white men's arrival.

"We come in peace", assured the captain, taking in the unwelcoming expression of the Ovie, whose support he so desperately needed now. "We have not come to fight against you—we have come to fight your battle. When my countrymen last visited your people, they were asked to respond to your most pressing concerns with the Edo—you told us that you desired free trade with these people, and this is the reason we are attacking them today. As soon as we can penetrate the land we will open it up so that free trade can recommence."

"You are not asking for us to give you men to help you fight the Edo are you?" the Ovie responded warily. "Because that would be impossible—those people are invincible. Although from what I have heard about your people, I think you may stand a chance. Nonetheless, please keep us out of this."

"We do not need your men", said the captain. "We have more than enough. All we need is to be shown alternative routes into the land so that we may surprise them."

The Ovie contemplated this for a while, his eyes darting from one British soldier to another as if to ascertain their trustworthiness. Finally, he leant forward and spoke in a lowered tone. "I will send someone to go with you but he must not be seen. He will point out the direction you need from afar, and then he will return to me. Is that acceptable to you?"

"That is perfectly acceptable", said the captain, getting to his feet. "We will need to make a move now because my men are still out there".

And so the Ovie sent a young man to accompany the small group of British soldiers, and instructed him to show them the other routes into the Benin kingdom.

On returning to base, the British captain gathered his troops, and, pacing up and down with his hands clasped behind his back, bellowed out his new commands. "It has been twelve days since we began this operation to wipe the Benin kingdom from the map, and we promised to complete the mission within a day from the launch of our attack. It has dragged on for too long, and I have lost too many men—far more than I had anticipated. Having studied the positioning of the Edo soldiers, I can see that the main entrance is well fortified and we might end up losing more men if we rely on this point alone. I have spoken to the ruler of the neighbouring village, and as a result I now know another way into the land. We need to divide the troop: we will leave a few men here to distract the enemy, and the main company will follow me to the other entrance. Here we will strike with heavy artillery. I am convinced that we can only overcome this voodoo-infested land by using the element of surprise."

Meanwhile, the soldiers from the Benin camp were all fighting courageously. They had been split into three groups, which were led by Ugowe, Asako, and General Eboigbe. The presence of these three great fighters had boosted their confidence to even greater heights; now each man stood smiling with pride whilst staring death straight in the face. This attitude towards battle was unfathomable to the British, who could not work out why the Edo soldiers were not afraid of guns. It even seemed as if some of these native fighters were wearing invisible, bullet-proof vests, as shots were ricocheting from many of their naked torsos without penetrating the flesh, although others fell down dead after just one hit.

CHAPTER 15

An Unexpected Event

DESPITE THE CLATTER of guns, harrowing screams, and scenes of carnage, the Edo refused to lose their focus and stuck rigidly to the commands of the three leaders. As was customary, they would dance and sing war songs before rushing forward to attack the invaders, who in turn would run backwards at their approach. Using this method, the Edo slaughtered as many of the British soldiers as they were able to reach, although some were lost to the many bullets that whistled incessantly through the air.

Asako and his men were right at the front line, close to where the British troops had built their camp. Relentlessly they stormed forward, attacking the invaders again and again, felling them like rotten trees with their machetes, and getting closer to the enemy camp with every charge. As they hurtled forwards yet again, this time with a real possibility of taking the British base, a terrific boom stopped them in their tracks, throwing them to the ground with the sheer force of the blast. An eerie, prolonged silence ensued. The air was thick with dust and smoke, making the men blind and disorientated. The odd shout or moan began to pierce through the smog, building gradually into an unsettling crescendo. As each surviving warrior slowly lifted his head from the dusty ground to look around in bewilderment at what had just happened, each was greeted with the sight of severed limbs and other human body parts that were scattered across the bloodied soil where they lay. With the dust now dissipating, several men clambered back to their feet and began looking around, desperately awaiting the command that would tell them what to do next.

But the command never came. Asako's body lay twisted on the front edge of the battleground, seemingly motionless other than the slight movement of his lips as he mumbled his final prayer. *Eki, my love. I have fulfilled my promise to you. I have wrestled the best fighter in Benin in front of my king, and I remained standing. Now I die fighting alongside him as his equal, and finally I come to join you my love, never to leave you again.* As Asako's lips fell still for the last time, the blood that had been seeping from the gaping wound in his stomach slowly trickled down onto the dry, dusty earth of Benin.

Finally, the Edo soldiers were scared. Those that were able to made a hasty retreat, chased by the crashing vibrations of another explosion, and then another, as the British fired canon after canon. Many of Asako's men had been killed, and as news of this great man's death spread within the troop the rest of the soldiers began to flee, as they had believed Asako to be immortal because of the charms he possessed.

Meanwhile, the main British troop had reached the other entrance to the kingdom, and from here they fired another canon towards the palace. A huge Iroko tree was caught in the blast, causing it to crash to the ground just feet away from the king's courtyard. The few chiefs that had remained in the palace came rushing out, anxious to learn what could create such a tremendous noise, and on seeing the devastation that had been caused by the British canon they were overcome with fear and so fled, deserting their king.

By now the British troops had gained full entry to the kingdom and were killing any man they saw. Even some of the women and children fell victim to stray bullets and over-zealous soldiers.

The news of Asako's death soon spread to the palace, disheartening the king greatly as he now realised that his army had been severely weakened. And when Osaro overheard the messenger relaying this dreadful information to the king, he had to keep his composure in order to keep Oghogho's revelation a secret. But as soon as he was able to secure a moment in private he wept bitterly, full of regret that he had never been able to meet his father and introduce himself to him as his son.

As sorrow slowly transformed to anger, Osaro strode up to the king who was sitting alone, cradling his head in his hands. "My lord, the time has come for me to fulfil my destiny", he said, his voice full of uncontrollable passion. "The chiefs have all deserted you, leaving you alone here in the palace. Release me so that I may join the battle, I beg of you. I will give our enemy a fight like they have never seen before."

The king looked up and smiled sadly at the young lad standing before him. His tone was weary, like that of an old man. "Osaro, you don't need to be deceptive. If you must, run and protect your own life. In fact I advise you to do this, and I promise I will not hold it against you. This war was caused by the chiefs, all of whom have now deserted me, but you have stood by my side all this time. So run before the enemy find you here and take your life for something you are not guilty of".

Osaro stood firm. "My king, I do not seek to protect my own life. I am going to fight because it is my destiny".

"Okay", said the king, who had no strength to argue. "You are free to go."

Without a moment's hesitation the boy ran to his room, whereupon he grabbed a machete, a bow, and a multitude of arrows before sprinting from the palace gates in search of the invaders.

As he made his way through the once bustling streets that now contained only lifeless bodies strewn about like litter, he came across a small boy who sat weeping. Next to him were the bloodied corpses of both his parents. Slowing down to a walk Osaro approached the child, who he guessed could be no more than thirteen years old. "It is wrong what the invaders have done", he said, placing a hand gently on the boy's shoulder. "I will make them pay for this". The boy raised his head to look at Osaro for the first time, his eyes deadened with grief.

"Would you like to see your parents' death avenged?" Osaro continued, and immediately the orphaned boy nodded his head.

"Very well", said Osaro. "You will have to come with me. How courageous are you?" he added.

"Very courageous", the boy whispered.

Osaro handed the rusty old machete to the child. "Take this, and listen carefully. Whenever you see me fall dead to the ground, use this machete to strike my corpse, and I will regain life. Can you do that for me?"

The boy nodded.

Arising to their feet, they turned to see hoards of terrified people running past them towards the borders of the kingdom, desperately trying to escape from the chaos within its walls. Side by side, the two boys started to walk in the opposite direction.

Meanwhile, Ugowe and General Eboigbe were still fighting in an attempt to ward the invaders back from the main entrance. The battle had become more intense as the Edo had fewer men, and those that remained had lost their courage following the news of Asako's death. Eboigbe turned to address Ugowe, his masculine face etched with concern. "I have noticed that the British soldiers have reduced in number, and yet we have not killed as many as are missing. You will need to take your men deeper into the land to see what is happening, and to make sure my king is being protected. The chiefs should be with him as I speak. Go at once, and bring word back to me as soon as possible!"

Ugowe gathered his men immediately, and together they headed into the kingdom. As they drew nearer to the palace, they saw that the whole place was in complete chaos, with people running for the borders in fear of their lives. All were too terrified to stop and talk to Ugowe, who was thus forced to seize a woman as she tried to run past. Giving her a quick shake in an attempt to bring her to her senses, he bellowed in her ear. "Woman! Tell me what is happening! Why is everyone in such panic? We have so far prevented the British from entering the land—there is no cause for such alarm as this!"

The woman looked back at him as if he were insane, her features contorted with a mixture of confusion and fear. "You prevented who from entering the land?" she screeched. "The white men are already here with their huge guns! They are killing everyone they see! We know they have killed Asako, and now all the chiefs have fled the palace, leaving the king alone to await his fate! How can you say that this is not enough to cause panic?"

Releasing the woman from his grasp, Ugowe watched her set off towards the borders. "Send word of this news to the General at once", he commanded, turning to a couple of his men. "Let him know that we have all been tricked—the British have already gained entry to our kingdom."

Then, having instructed a small section of his company to protect the palace, he set out with the rest in search of the invaders.

CHAPTER 16

Osaro Takes A Stand

O SARO, MEANWHILE, HAD already located the main point of invasion and had been engaged in battle with the enemy for some time. His tactics was far more efficient than those who had been fighting with machetes; using just his bow and arrow he had killed a large number of men single-handedly. Now the British were in a state of panic; they could not understand how Osaro was still alive despite being shot repeatedly. All they could do was to keep shooting and retreating, whilst the boy continued to drop their men one after another.

This was the scene that greeted Ugowe and his men as they reached the location of the invaders. Having seen what the young warrior had achieved, Ugowe was in awe of how a little palace boy could possess such powers, but was also aware that there was no time to waste on pleasantries and questions. He signalled for Osaro to step back, and then he and his men charged towards the invaders. His plan was to gain advantage by engaging the enemy in close combat, as this was the type of warfare that the Edo warriors were experienced in. Sadly, this proved to be a serious mistake. Recognising the approaching onslaught, the British captain ordered the canon to be fired—and this was the same type of canon that had destroyed the mighty Asako. The explosion wiped out the majority of Ugowe's men, leaving the remainder—including Ugowe himself—suffering from unthinkable injuries.

On hearing that the British were already deep within the land and that the king was now alone, General Eboigbe was overwhelmed with anger and immediately set off in the direction of the palace. As he marched, he vowed to kill every single chief for causing the war and daring to abandon the king.

A couple of chiefs that he passed on his way were instantly felled without question, as were any invaders that crossed his path. As his fury grew, however, he began to lose focus, and it was not long before he was captured by the British.

Meanwhile, the soldiers that been left to defend the entrance of the kingdom had long since fled for their lives, and now the enemy was rapidly advancing from both ends.

Osaro, on the other hand, was fighting for all his worth, whilst the little boy to whom he had given the old machete was hiding nearby, watching the whole event.

The British captain had also been studying Osaro as he fought. After a while, he called out to some of his officers. "I don't think that this young lad is fighting alone. I believe he has some strong forces surrounding him, so what we should do is to direct the canon at him".

The soldiers immediately did as they were instructed. As the canon ball hit Osaro it scattered his flesh all over the ground, and instantly it was clear that the brave young fighter was dead. The little boy quickly ran out of his hiding place, brandishing the machete, ready to strike the remains of the corpse, but a closer look at the torn body parts made his stomach churn with fear. Petrified, he threw away the machete and fled, scared for his own life.

"This animal was a tough cookie", said one of the British soldiers as they approached the Osaro's body. "He gave us a lot of hell."

"I don't know how these bastards get such powers", said another, wiping the steaming sweat from his forehead with the back of his hand.

As they got closer to the shredded corpse, one of the soldiers made a beeline for Osaro's hand, which had been severed from the wrist and now lay ominously on the ground, still clutching the bow.

"Bloody animal thought he was invincible", he growled, kicking it insolently with his right foot.

At this contact, Osaro's body began joining together. As the soldiers stared on in amazement, their eyes growing wider by the second and their feet frozen to the spot where they stood, Osaro jumped up and started attacking them with his arrows and spears. This time he killed twice as many, as they were so horror-stricken they just stumbled around aimlessly in an attempt to run away.

The captain had to reorganise the men himself, so in shock were they. Once back in formation they just stood there with their jaws gaping, trying to work out if this was a human or ghost that was attacking them now.

"Shoot him again with the canon!" the captain bellowed.

As the fearsome machine was pointed directly at Osaro for a second time, a shout of "FIRE!" reverberated through the smoky air and an almighty explosion followed. Once again, Osaro was blown into a multitude of pieces, but this time the soldiers stood far away from his remains, terrified that he may stand up for a second time.

The captain ordered seven of his most trustworthy men to guard the corpse, making sure that nothing came into contact with it, before setting off with the rest of his army.

As the troops headed deeper into the land they were met with no further opposition—all of the native fighters had now fled. Before long they were marching through the doors of the palace, whereupon they suddenly stopped dead in their tracks. The huge amount of treasure possessed by the Edo was now staring them in the face.

All at once the soldiers threw themselves onto the riches like a pack of starving wolves.

"Captain! See this!" shouted one of the men, holding up a bronze casting that bore the face of a beautiful woman.

"Gather it all together, for we will take the spoils of this land", the captain replied, his eyes glistening with greed.

Without any hesitation, the soldiers helped themselves to all of the wood and ivory carvings, and the furs of lions, leopards, tigers, and other animals. They also took tons of religious artefacts, bronze castings, and precious ornaments, including corals.

And when they came upon the king who was hiding within the palace, they seized him, and barraged him with taunts.

"You're not so tough now are you?" jeered one, spitting into his face. "See you at the trial, your not so royal highness".

CHAPTER 17

The Trial

O N THE DAY of the trial a huge crowd had gathered. All of the people of Benin were hoping that their king would be released, and that they would be allowed to live in peace. There were armed soldiers all around as the British were not going to take anything for granted; they knew how much the Edo loved their king, and seeing him go through trial might spark off violence, they thought.

The king tried hard to tell his own side of the story; he tried to make his persecutors understand that he did not order the killing of the British visitors; but his explanation fell on deaf ears, and shouts and insults kept drowning out his words.

"Why is he still wearing a crown?" a skinny soldier cried out.

"Make him kneel and beg for forgiveness!" yelled another.

"Strip him off any pride he may have left!" jeered a third, his face twisted with contempt.

"You heard him!" hissed the consul general. "Now kneel!"

At this there was uproar from the crowd, and the soldiers charged towards the people to restrain them.

One of the chiefs who had previously abandoned the king took the opportunity to step forward. "It is forbidden for a king to kneel down!" he exclaimed. "This has never been and will never be! Please do not make us break our tradition! You have heard the king swear that he was not responsible for the violence, and I can testify to that."

"Silence!" shouted a large, red-faced gentleman who was sitting amongst those questioning the king. "He must kneel, otherwise ..."

"Otherwise what?" interrupted the king, no longer able to stay quiet. "Will you spill more blood than you already have? Will you take away any more than you already have?"

As the king continued to speak out, a gentle murmuring sound started to build within the crowd until it grew into a clamour that suggested the people were warming up for violence. The soldiers prepared to open fire, having been ordered to destroy the kingdom, kill the king, and burn everything at the slightest opportunity.

"Enough!" boomed the familiar baritone voice. The king was now standing, calling out to the crowd. "There shall be no more bloodshed. I have lost too many innocent people already! So my citizens, no more fighting!" he commanded.

The red-faced man spoke again. "Very well" he declared. "If you refuse to kneel then you will cease to be king."

"Or we could just force you to kneel anyway" said the British consul general, as he got up and made his way towards him. Then, stretching out his hand, he reached for the king's crown and snatched it from his head. Loud cries, wails, and screaming erupted from the crowd, startling the British who could not understand the strength of this reaction.

In order to distract from the noise, the red-faced man hastily jumped up and began reading out the verdict. "You are banished from this land", he cried at the top of his voice. The crowd gasped, and then resumed their wailing.

The king looked straight at the British consul general, his face full of dignity and pride. "I am king of Benin kingdom", he said, speaking slowly as if to a very young child. "The gods made me king—I have not given myself this honour. You put your dirty hand on my head because you have no respect for the gods. That same hand that you used to touch my crown you will use to take your own life."

The British consul general merely laughed at this curse, and standing with his arms folded watched the king being led out of Benin, never to return again.

CHAPTER 18

A Spiritual Happening

SEVEN DAYS AFTER the battle ended, a handful of soldiers were still sitting around Osaro's remains, ensuring that nothing was able to touch them. Now that their fear had faded they were becoming bored and had begun swopping jokes and tall stories. Suddenly, one of the men put his finger to his lips and cocked his head to one side.

"Shh! Listen!" he whispered, and as they all sat in silence a faint cheeping noise could be heard. Suddenly, seven little chicks appeared as if in convoy, walking in a straight line like soldiers.

The British men watched with wide eyes and hanging jaws, clueless as to the meaning of this strange occurrence. Then, as quickly as they had appeared, the chicks vanished.

The soldiers jumped up and ran back to their captain, describing what had just happened in a jumble of words and gasps. The captain was silent for a moment before ordering the men to follow him back to where Osaro lay.

On reaching the spot, the captain bent down and picked up one of the arrows that lay on the ground, stained in blood. As soon as the soldiers saw that contact had been made with one of the boy's possessions, they staggered backwards in horror, waiting for the strange being to stand up and attack as he had done before. The captain, however, calmly removed his cap and held it to his chest, and then positioned himself with one knee to the ground. Watching the boy carefully, he knelt in this way for what seemed like thirty minutes.

Eventually he called out to his soldiers, who were still ready to run at the slightest sign of movement from the dismembered corpse, and ordered them to gather the bloodied parts.

"He deserves to be buried properly", muttered the captain, still not taking his eyes from the boy's face, and quietly admiring the brevity of the young lad—not to mention the strange powers he possessed.

When the British soldiers had finally finished burying the body parts, the captain announced that the event they had witnessed earlier was confirmation that Osaro had at that moment passed away. *What a man!* he thought to himself, as he marked the grave with a black, wooden cross that he had personally made. On it were the words, '*He Was A Man*'.

Three Months Later

Having been completely taken over by the British, the Benin kingdom had gradually begun to settle down. Now that it was safe for a young maiden to venture across the land, Oghogho made her way to the spot where Osaro was buried, and kneeling beside his grave, she began to cry. "Osaro, my love, I told you that if I broke the vow then I would never get married, but you did not listen. I tried to warn you that the gods are never wrong. You promised to marry me. Now that you have left me alone in this world, is it in the afterlife that we will be married? Osaro, my love, you did not keep your promise, but I understand that death cannot separate us". Sobbing with grief, she leant forward and kissed the little black cross that marked the grave. "You always wanted to be a warrior and now you have fulfilled your dream, despite the fact that no one believed it would happen. From the first day I saw you, I knew you were a warrior but I did not want you to take that path because it always leads to such a tragic end. I wanted you to be a loving father. That was my choice for you" she whispered, gently rubbing her stomach. "Rest now, Osaro my love. Rest in peace until we meet again". Kissing the wooden cross for a second time she rose to her feet, her hands still cradling her rounded stomach.

EPILOGUE

$\mathcal{T}$HE KING OF Benin lived out the rest of his years as an ordinary person in a foreign land. This was a punishment the British thought would be suitably painful; they were not allowed to execute him for political reasons, but they needed him out of the way so that they could carry out their original plan of making the kingdom a British colony. However, with the kingdom now in ruins, all they were really interested in was looting.

The captured soldiers, including Ugowe and General Eboigbe, and the chiefs who ordered the massacre of the British visitors, were all sentenced to death by hanging.

Many years later, the British consul general—who had become exceedingly wealthy and famous as a result of his success in taking over the Benin kingdom—was relaxing in his home, when he suddenly began to see images of strange-looking people, all of whom appeared to be staring at him. As he was alone in these visions, he knew better than to share what was happening with anyone else for fear of people thinking that he had lost his mind. Petrified, he tried to escape the hallucinations by running from room to room, but they followed him wherever he went, their dark, menacing eyes permanently on his. On realising that one of the faces was exactly the same as an artefact stolen from the Benin palace, he began to tremble uncontrollably. *Could these be the Benin gods I am seeing?* he thought to himself. *Or could it be the king's curse?* As panic took over his mind, one of the ghoulish faces swooped inches away from his own. Immediately, his body became paralysed; try as he might, he was unable to move any of his limbs. From nowhere, one of his own hands reached up towards his neck, grabbing it fiercely and tightening its grip second by second. Frantically the consul general tried to prise the fingers open with his other hand, but as his lungs became starved of air his efforts became weaker and weaker, until finally he collapsed to the floor. The ghostly faces were now fading, and in their place was the image of the king's crown lying on the ground. Two minutes later, there was nothing.

His body was discovered by a steward who had come to serve him drinks.

An autopsy was carried out in order to ascertain the cause of death, but nothing could explain the mystery. Therefore, it was concluded that the consul general committed suicide, but questions were raised as to whether this was mere coincidence or rather a result of the curse of the mighty Benin king. Or could it be that the stolen artefacts, such as the ivory, were carrying the curse?

THE END